UNTO THE LEAST OF THESE

DOUGLAS ALAN

ARPress
ILLUMINATING IDEAS
EMPOWERING VOICES

ARPress
45 Dan Road Suite 5
Canton MA 02021

Hotline: 1(800) 220-7660
Fax: 1(855) 752-6001

Ordering Information:
Quantity sales. Special discounts are available on quantity purchases by corporations, associations, and others. For details, contact the publisher at the address above.

Printed in the United States of America.

ISBN-13:   Paperback   979-8-89389-385-4
              eBook   979-8-89389-386-1

Library of Congress Control Number: 2024916614

To my son, Bryan, who inspired this
story and left us far too early.

CHAPTER 1

Dan Pearson, tall and strong from years of physical work, leaned on a wooden rail fence in central California with his preteen daughter, Carrie, watching the carefree play among four young horses as they ran, kicked, and chased one another around the pasture.

"Dad," Carrie remarked, "they like it. They're so free and can do what they want. But they aren't. They're contained in the fence."

"You know, Carrie, we're just like them." Dan smiled down at the girl. "In life, we are free, but we're also controlled by fences. Our boundaries are made of what is right and wrong, moral and immoral, accepted and not accepted. We see on the news every day about stores being robbed, people killed, drug arrests, and all the problems this world seems to have. Many of these acts of wrongdoing are because so many people live for themselves and what they want or need and not being part of society and asking, 'How can I make life better for everyone?'"

After watching the energetic horses for a while longer without speaking, Carrie asked, "Why do you have to go to Denver now, Dad?"

Dan sighed, "There are still some parts of your mother's estate that aren't settled. I've got to handle them in person. The attorneys, accountants, and bankers—all feel we can achieve much more if we are all together in one room rather than the current way of sending messages back and forth to each other. This is all because even though we don't have great wealth, your mother's family was very successful in many different business ventures, so her death has brought proposed changes to her estate plans."

"Do you miss Mom?"

He put his arm around her shoulders. "There is not a day that goes by that I don't think of her because each time I look at you, I see her." With her olive skin and beautiful black eyes, the girl was the image of her mother.

Carrie leaned affectionately against her father. "I know it's been more than three years, but it still seems like the funeral was yesterday."

He squeezed her shoulders. "Yes, it does."

"How long will you be gone?"

"Just overnight. I'll drive to LA early tomorrow morning to catch an 11:00 a.m. flight to Denver. I'll meet with the attorneys on Tuesday morning and come right back that evening. Come on."

They strolled down the path toward the house, arms lovingly around each other.

He reminded her, "You'll be fine with Jose and Tina."

She smiled, "I know. They are just like our family, aren't they?"

"They are our family. When I was growing up, Jose was like my older brother."

Carrie nodded. She knew. Her father had told her many times about the bond between the two men.

Dan added, "He's always been here, helping my parents and now working with me."

Carrie asked, "Why did they never have children, Dad? I would have had friends my age to play with."

While Dan pondered how to answer that question the right way, he simply said, "Some married couples just can't have a baby for medical reasons." He continued, "I know they talked about a family years ago, but guess they just adopted us instead!"

Carrie seemed content with that response.

Thinking about what her dad had said about people's fences, Carrie wondered, "Do you think Tina and Jose believe they're free?"

Dan nodded, "Yes, I do because they come and go as they want. They're here without having to worry where they'd live or where their money will come from. So, yes, they have chosen their own fences by deciding how far they go before they return."

This girl of mixed race with olive skin and beautiful black eyes looked up into her father's eyes and said, "I've already chosen my fence. I want to live here forever on this ranch."

Dan shook his head with a smile. "You'll have to travel outside this fence when the time comes to receive your advanced education, Carrie. You need to examine life beyond these boundaries."

"But I don't want to leave ever!"

"But when the time comes, you will, young lady. You will." She thought of that for some time and decided that her father was just wrong. She could never leave.

The next morning at daybreak, Dan quietly opened the door to Carrie's room and peeked in. She was sleeping soundly, so he shut the door. He put his coffee cup in the sink, picked up his overnight bag, and walked out to his pickup. Jose was leaning on the box. Dan told him again, "I'll be home tomorrow night. Take care of Carrie until I get back."

"*Hermano*, Brother, don't worry. As always, I'll take care of her as a daughter of my own."

Dan knew as he climbed into the pickup that truer words were never spoken. Jose would indeed watch her as he had since she was brought home from the hospital as a baby.

It was one of those perfect California mornings, a little cool with a promise of a sunshine-filled day in the eighties. The reason so many people called this beautiful state home.

The drive to Los Angeles that morning gave Dan Pearson time to reflect on his life: finding the girl of his dreams while in college, marrying after receiving his degree in architecture, working in town while settling in with his bride in the guesthouse on the small ranch he grew up on with his parents nearby. And he had been thinking life just could not get any better, finding a woman that had the same beliefs and wants in life as he did, sharing in the joy of their first and only child, a beautiful little girl, his parents nearby to help guide and be a part of his family.

All seemed perfect until that day he received a call at work. His young wife of twenty some years had been rushed to the hospital after a serious car crash. As he had so many times since then, Pearson remembered his rush to the hospital and the fears flooding through his mind. What if he lost this one person who meant everything to him? She was not only his wife but best friend. He'd raced into the hospital only to find out as he got to the hospital that they were unable to save her. She was dead. How could his life continue without her? In despair, he had thought, *How can I go on*? But even as he asked that question, he knew he must for their young daughter.

As those thoughts flooded his memory, it did seem like he'd suffered the loss only yesterday. How many times had he relived that terrible day and being told that the love of his life was gone? How many times he had asked himself what he could have done or said so she was not in that spot on the road at that time? And how many times had he wished he could have told her one last time how much he loved her and cared for her? As he reflected on Carrie, how much she not only looked like her mother but how often many of her actions mirrored her mothers. Dan smiled. Then he concentrated on finding a parking place in the jungle of cars, asphalt, and people at LAX.

CHAPTER 2

As he approached the passenger drop-off area, Dan saw a beautiful woman in her late thirties exiting a limo. He recognized her as an actress or singer or someone he'd seen on TV. He did not know her name or really what she did as those kinds of things were not very important to him. He rarely watched TV and had no interest in reading about the intimate details of such media stars that seemed plastered everywhere. He did enjoy an occasional movie now and then and wondered to himself when was the last time he and his lovely wife, Annie, had been to a movie before she died? And then, he wondered when was the last time he and Carrie had had a date night to a movie? Dan made a mental note to get that done when he returned.

As he continued to watch this entourage, carrying bags and suitcases, three members scurried after her as she made her way toward the luggage outdoor check-in stand. Yes, she was striking, wearing that full length white/gray mink coat.

He thought it was odd as it was going to be a nice day, but the morning air did have a crisp feel to it, being late fall.

The line of people, waiting to check in, slowed their progress to a crawl, and the famous-looking woman stopped in the middle of the crowded sidewalk to light a cigarette. A homeless old woman and her shopping cart full of odds and ends was waiting to cross the busy street in front of the terminal. As the men with the celebrity's luggage were pushing through and trying to get around other passengers, they accidentally knocked the old woman and her cart off the sidewalk and into the driveway. Rather than helping her, all three laughed and continued moving away through the crowd from the old woman, lying in a heap next to her overturned cart. Looking at this poor woman, now with old dirty clothes and shoes that did not seem to fit just right, was surely someone's little girl at one time, someone who had hopes and dreams. How does a life start with so much hopes and dreams come down to this poor woman, lying in the street?

Cars in that lane stopped. Some honked. Dan immediately walked down to her and knelt beside this small frail woman. Apparently unhurt, she was struggling to get up, so he helped her to her feet. He set her cart back up on its wheels, picked a tattered quilt and a bulging black garbage bag up off the pavement, and stuffed them back into her cart on top of her other belongings. Setting his overnight bag on top, he offered his left arm to hang onto. As she clung to it, he guided her across the busy street, pushing her cart with his right hand.

As he helped her and the cart up onto the opposite sidewalk, Dan asked, "Are you hurt?" as he retrieved his overnight bag.

"Only my pride, sir." The small woman shakily reached up to pull his head down so she could kiss his cheek. "Thank you. May our lovely Lord always walk with you." She gave him a shaky smile and pushed her cart away.

As he walked back across the busy drive-through area, Dan was thinking about what she had said to him, and those words stayed on his mind.

"Hey, if I were you, I'd go get that cheek disinfected," one of the celebrity's helpers commented to Dan, and the little group laughed. Pearson ignored them.

The baggage attendant at the check-in kiosk was ticketing the luggage of the celebrity. As she started away toward the nearby entrance, the man cautioned her, "Ma'am, no smoking in the terminal."

"Nobody tells me what I can do!" She snapped back over her shoulder. "I'll do what I want."

The attendant took a few steps after her. "Ma'am, you can't smoke in there. I'll have to call security."

One of the woman's minions touched her shoulder. "Come on, Eva," he coaxed. "You know full well. You can't smoke in there. The flight's only a couple of hours. Have a cocktail or two. You can go that long without a cigarette."

Now Dan knew why the woman looked familiar. She was a movie actress, Eva St. Clair, a star with a reputation for *difficult* behavior. He shook his head as he looked at the spoiled beautiful woman. She was obviously all wrapped up in her own life without any consideration for anyone around her or their wants, feelings, or needs.

The world she lives in isn't real, he thought. *She's got no idea what life can be.*

As he walked through the terminal to find his gate, he followed the procession of Ms. St. Clair and her entourage. She was complaining nonstop about everything from having to walk such a distance, to needing a cigarette, to wanting something to eat. When one of her assistants offered to get her something, she rudely dismissed all his suggestions.

Total disregard for anyone around her, thought Dan. *Everything's about her.* He was dismayed to see her enter the same gate waiting area he was going into. *Great, she's flying to Denver too.*

The actress immediately ordered the gate attendant to let her go down the gateway to have a cigarette. When the attendant naturally refused, Eva St. Clair loudly told the woman what she thought of her for denying this small request. Dan could feel his dislike of the rude and uncaring woman becoming stronger.

He wondered, *How a person could become so self-centered on one-self? Does everyone want to be around you to touch you, to just be near you have that effect on a person overtime? Guess I will never know the answer to that question.*

Later as they boarded the plane, it was again all about her and her seating. Everyone had to wait for her to get settled in first class so the line could pass into the economy cabin. As they waited to taxi and takeoff, her voice filled the plane with nonstop complaining about how long it was taking, how hot the plane was, how bad the seats were, etc.

Dan did his best to tune out her voice and let his thoughts return to his quiet ranch, his loving daughter, and the life he cherished so much. He was ready to leave this surreal world of plastic, people, and things.

As the plane at last made its way to the runway and took off, he thought to himself, *Finally, get this thing going, get to Denver, get the meeting over. Then back to my world as soon as possible.*

About an hour into the flight, the pilot came on the intercom to explain that there was a major winter storm over the front range of Utah and western Colorado. He said they would try to skirt it to the south. Once they cleared those mountains, all was well in Denver.

Shortly after this announcement, there was a loud noise as if something had hit the plane. It shook violently from side to side then started to descend. Passengers were yelling and sobbing when the copilot spoke on the intercom, "Folks, it appears we have lost one of our engines and parts of it may have hit the underside of the wing. The captain is unable to hold the plane level, and we're losing elevation. We've asked the nearest airport for clearance to land. Everyone please remain calm."

The plane shook again, worse than before, and oxygen masks dropped from above. Over the pounding of his heart in his ears and the shouting and crying of other passengers, Dan could hear the beautiful actress in first class, demanding the cabin attendant's attention. She shrilly made it clear how she felt about the airline, the crew, and all the terrified passengers around her.

The plane was losing elevation fast. Pearson looked out the window and saw the sunlight disappear as they plunged into dark clouds. Again, the copilot came on and announced the pilot couldn't hold the plane steadily until they reached an airport. He ordered everyone to make sure their seatbelts were secure, bend over, and hold on as they were going to attempt a crash landing.

Thoughts were flooding his mind, wondering if he had seen his lovely Carrie for the last time, the little ranch he loved, his parents, Jose, and Tina. And was he now about to join his wife again? All these things passed through his mind as the plane bounced hard on the ground.

Dan turned his head on his knees and took a peek out the window. Snow streamed past. He thought he saw a faint light. Then everything went black as the plane started breaking up. Part of the back plane, just behind his row, broke off. People cried and screamed they were going to die. From his huddled position, Dan watched as the front of the plane just tore off and went sideways. At that point, he felt the main fuselage started to flip over. His head slammed against something, and everything went black.

CHAPTER 3

Pearson woke up hanging sideways in his seat. For some reason, some lights were still on in this crumpled portion of the plane. The whole thing was tilted at a steep angle. As he fumbled to undo his seatbelt, pain stabbed his shoulder and back.

His chin hurt, and blood from it dripped onto his hand.

Other than the howling of the wind, there were no sounds. The remaining lights went out. All Dan could see in the dim light were bodies and bloodied metal and glass. He peered around, trying to find the best way out. Slowly he made his way toward what had been the front of the plane, clambering over bodies and seats and luggage everywhere. As he looked at the dead around him, he realized how lucky he was to be alive. Now he needed to get out and survive.

As he crawled forward, he heard moaning. He moved past luggage and bodies to reach the sound. Sprawled in front of him was Eva St. Clair, and she was alive. He reached to touch her. All of a sudden, the plane violently tipped forward at a steeper angle. People and bags slid past them as he grabbed a seat with one hand and held onto the actress with the other. She began to slip forward. He could see through the open front of the plane that they were on the edge of a canyon. Whatever had stopped this part of the cabin as it was about to go over held it hanging there on the brink.

The moaning actress slid further along the floor. Dan felt himself being pulled along as everything he grasped with his free hand was breaking loose. As a last ditch effort before they fell to their certain death, he swung his right leg out to catch it on something he saw sticking up. Immense pain jolted him as the object ripped into his leg, but it did stop their slide.

He lay there, barely held by his leg, and clutched this unpleasant woman. Pearson thought, *What am I doing? She's barely alive. I've just got to let go and save myself. Why should I risk my life trying to save her?* But because of how he was raised, he acted on his lifelong instinct to help anyone in need. He hung on.

As he gradually pulled his burden back up to where he could get both hands on her, he was able to wedge the actress behind a seemingly secure though broken seat. Then he tried to get his leg off the object that had been holding both of them. As he pulled his leg back, the severe pain and the warm liquid, running down it, told him he was bleeding badly.

As he tried to lift the helpless woman, she cried out in pain with every movement. Again, he asked himself, "Why am I doing this? She wouldn't in a lifetime help me!" Somehow, he found the strength to half drag, half carry her back up toward his seat. As he passed where she had been seated, there was that beautiful mink coat wedged under a seat. He grabbed it, thinking with the cold air it would be needed.

The plane seemed to quiver with his movements. He stuck his head out of a large hole to be met with a blast of terrible wind driven snow and severe cold. Despite the weather, he knew they had to get out of the section of plane before it shifted again and plummeted into the canyon.

As he looked around in the dim light, he saw the back edge of the torn plane and a possible exit to the outside. As he pulled the unconscious woman through the hole with him, he collapsed and for a few minutes just lay on the icy hard ground. Feeling more and more drowsy, he forced himself to move. Remembering the injury to his leg, he looked around. Just inside the cavity of the plane he saw a shirt. He grabbed it and managed to rip the sleeves off. He wrapped them in two layers around his bleeding leg as tightly as he could and knotted them.

As he pulled his companion a few yards, the plane behind them began slipping again. In a minute, it was completely gone. Realizing his luck, he exclaimed, "Thank you, Lord!" And thought again what the homeless woman had said to him, "Walk with the Lord."

He lay there, holding onto the woman, and knew they were going to freeze to death on that spot. The cold was so severe it just drove right through his body. He was not dressed for winter weather, just a light fall or spring coat and long sleeve western cut shirt. Grabbing the mink coat, he wrapped it around her as best he could and lifted her up, started walking away.

Then he remembered the faint light he had seen just before the crash. Raising his head and looking all around in the blinding snowstorm, he could see nothing. Having always had an instinct for knowing which direction to go, being raised in the country, he struggled to lift the woman in his arms. Each movement caused her to cry out. He again thought, *What are you doing? Just set her down here. Try and save yourself. Find shelter somewhere.* But something would not allow him to let her go. He kept stumbling forward through the snow and wind and severe cold until he could no longer carry her or even keep himself moving forward. He simply could not carry her and walk through this deep snow and go on. He thought to himself, *If only I had a sled, I could pull her over the snow.*

As he ran that through his mind, looking down at this woman in his arms so hurt, so lost, wrapped in a coat worth thousands of dollars, just then the coat hit his mind. He sat her on the frozen cold snow and unwrapped the coat around her, spreading it on the snow. He laid her on it and buttoned the front, lifting the arms up and over her head. He started pulling, and to his joy, that fancy mink coat slid wonderfully over the snow.

After what seemed like forever, he slumped to the ground on his knees, still holding the coat and Eva St. Clair. *What a way to end my life here in the middle of nowhere. In a snowstorm, holding a woman who'd never have lifted a hand to help me or anybody else.* He drifted in and out of consciousness. Once, when he came to, he realized the snow had stopped blowing in his face. In that clear moment, he thought he saw the faint light he'd glimpsed from the plane. He peered at it and wondered, *Is that light real? Am I dreaming?*

Dan again felt himself falling asleep. He shook his head and his arms and forced himself to get up. As he staggered to his feet with the woman dragging behind, she again cried out. He began slogging through even heavier snow toward where he remembered seeing that light. He couldn't see it anymore through the snow that was again swirling about him, but he kept trudging forward. A voice in his head said, "There's no light. You imagined it." Just as he was ready to believe that voice and drop to his knees and give up, the snow again let up briefly, and now he could clearly see a light in the distance.

He kept wading through the snow one step at a time, chanting to himself, "Just a little more, just a little more. Keep going. You can do it." All he wanted to do was to stop and lie down and sleep. But he made his legs keep moving until right in front of him appeared the front porch of a small log cabin.

He dragged himself and his load up to the door and never even stopped to knock. He simply fumbled it open and stumbled forward into a nice warm room. Before everything went dark for him, he remembered seeing a fire in the corner of the room. And then all was quiet.

Dan woke up shivering. The room was cold. The sound of the terrible wind outside told him the storm had worsened. He looked around and saw the dim light of a kerosene lantern on a small table. As he pushed himself to his feet, pain shot through his right leg. He groaned from that and from the injuries to his shoulder and back. He staggered toward the light.

Just as he reached the table, he saw a figure sitting in the chair beside it and reeled back in shock. After standing there and staring, he slowly moved forward again. He reached out to the lantern and turned the wheel that raised the wick and gave more light. The small cabin had the smell of burned wood, stale cigarette smoke, and musty air in its close quarters and human smell.

He could now clearly see a small elderly man, sitting motionless in the chair with his head tilted back. He reached out to touch the old man's cold cheek and realized he was dead. Logic told him the man must have died that day as there had been a fire burning, and the room had been warm. Dan carefully picked up the lantern and explored the small cabin, seeing cupboards above a countertop in the corner of the room. A door in one wall led into a small room with a regular toilet seat on a small bench and a pot below.

Like an indoor outhouse, he thought with a hint of a smile. *Won't have to go out in the storm to use the facilities.*

On the other side of the main room, he saw the old man, the table, a leather couch, and a big rock fireplace. Back to his left, the woman was lying, unmoving on the floor, still wrapped in her coat. He wondered if she, too, was dead, but as he knelt down to touch her, he could hear her shallow breathing.

The cold was beginning to go through him, so he limped to the fireplace where the fire had almost died out. With a few logs that were stacked beside it and some crumpled newspaper that he stuffed into the embers, he finally managed to get the fire going again. The actions reminded him sadly of how many times he'd done the same thing in his own home for just that extra warmth on a chilly evening. Yes, back home. How he wished he was there now.

It wasn't long before, the fire was going strong, and the room was again warming up. Dan tried to decide what to do next. He thought he remembered noticing a stack of firewood by the front door as he dragged himself in hours a day before, but he wasn't sure. He opened the door to face a large snowbank on the porch. Wobbling painfully on his bad leg, he kicked and cleared a path with his other one. When he stumbled against the firewood, he smiled grimly at his good luck. He lifted as many split logs as he could carry and hobbled with them to the fireplace. Three more trips made him feel he had enough wood to hold him for a while possibly until help could come. He thought of the old man and what the heat was going to do to his dead body. He was not a big man and quite old, he thought. He wondered about his life, his family.

As he placed the old man outside in the snowbank, Dan felt remorse. He had invaded this man's home and its warmth and now was removing him from his own home to lie in the cold.

CHAPTER 4

As he shut the door, his eyes fell on the woman, lying on the floor.

"What am I supposed to do with her?" he wondered. As he started toward her, his leg again throbbed with pain. He limped to the old man's chair and collapsed into it. He managed to untie the shirtsleeves he had bound around his leg. Wincing as the blood stiffened denim pulled on his leg, he slowly worked his jeans off. He peered down at the jagged cut across his inner thigh. His leg was matted with dried blood. He nodded. "Need to clean that."

Gazing around, he spotted a bucket on the counter in the corner and suddenly realized how thirsty he was. He walked over to see what was in the bucket and was startled by a movement in the opposite corner of that dim lit kitchen. What was it? He went and picked the lantern off the table, and walking back, he saw that it was a small dog all curled up and scared. As he reached down to touch its head, the poor dog just laid its head on the floor. He could tell the dog was himself old but appeared to be well taken care of.

He let him touch his head, and as he stroked his head, the little dog tried to lick his hand.

Remembering how thirsty he was, he stood up and turned back to the counter and found that the bucket was indeed half full of water. A large metal cup was hanging on the wall. As he dipped the cup and lifted it to his lips, he could hardly swallow. After guzzling three cups of water, Pearson felt somewhat refreshed.

Seeing movement by his feet, he turned to see the little dog had followed him and was just standing there, looking up at him. He decided the poor thing must also be thirsty, so opening a couple of cupboard doors, he finally found a small bowl and also saw a bag of dog food. Placing the bowl on the floor, he poured a cup of water into it, and the little bugger drank it all. He wondered then about where and how the dog did its bathroom habits and felt he should see if he wanted to go outside.

As he opened the door and again kicked snow out of the way, snow fell off the old man where he had laid him beside the door opposite from the firewood. The poor little fella walked out and, seeing his old master, walked over and laid his head on his lap. As Dan stared at this sight, his heart was heavy, seeing the love this animal had for what must have been his lifelong companion.

As he turned to go back in the cabin, he called for the dog to come, but just then, he jumped off the porch into the snow and disappeared. Dan stood there, calling out, but the dog did not come.

Great, he thought, *The old man's dead, and now his dog will surely freeze to death outside.* He closed the door against the terrible cold and again was grateful for the nice warmth of the fireplace.

He found a cloth folded on the counter and another bowl in one of the cupboards. He filled the bowl with water and sat down again in the chair to clean his wound. It was deep. *That needs stitches*, he thought. *But I'll just have to make the best of it until help comes.*

He got up again to look through the two cupboards to see what else was in there. His good luck was still with him. He found a bottle of hydrogen peroxide. *Sure, a man living by himself would have it around to clean any wounds he might suffer.* Dan poured peroxide on his thigh and watched as it foamed. *Yeah, already infection in there.* He dried the wound and found a clean-looking dish towel to tie around his leg. Then he carefully pulled his stiffened jeans back on.

Just as he was standing up, he heard a noise at the door and went to open it. There stood that little dog just wanting to come home. He let him in and watched as he shook himself off with snow flying everywhere from his long hair. Dan walked over to the cup-board, and getting the bag of dog food, he put some in the water bowl and watched as the poor little fella started to eat.

He finally made his way to where Eva St. Clair lay on the floor. With each movement as he lifted and carried her across the room to the couch, she cried out. In the light of the fireplace and the lantern, he could now see that her beautiful face had a nasty cut across the cheek and part of her lip. Her blouse and one pant leg were stiff with dried blood. He limped back over to the chair and sat there, thinking about her and her injuries. "Help will be here soon," he told himself. "They'll be looking for the plane."

But as he listened to the terrible wind buffeting the cabin, reality hit him. He knew while the storm continued, there would be no search for the plane. He couldn't leave her as she was. He had to find out what her injuries were.

Just then, the little dog walked over and laid down beside his chair and curled up. He wondered how many times he had done that over the years as surely that had been and was his *spot*.

He rinsed the rag he'd used on his own leg and took it, a bowl of water, and the peroxide bottle back to the couch. He stared down at the unconscious woman. "Maybe I'm wasting my time. She's been out for what? A day now? Maybe she'll never wake up. Anyway, why worry about a person who'd never have given me a second look?" But even as he thought about this, he knelt beside her motionless body and started dabbing at her cheek and forehead. As the dried, caked blood washed off, he could see more clearly the nasty cut, zigzagging across her cheek.

"She used to be such a beautiful woman. If she lives, how is she going to handle this new look?"

Dan poured the peroxide into the open cut and watched as it foamed up, doing its job of attacking infection. He could see that the jagged edges of the cut were already turning a different color. Meaning, the skin was ready to die and recede. It would leave a terrible scar. Maybe he could do something about it.

He limped back to the kitchen area and looked through the cupboards again. He found a few dishes, some cups, three cans of beans, part of a bag of crackers, and a jar of honey. A pang of hunger distracted him, and he thought, *When did I last eat?*

As he reached for the can of beans, he remembered Ms. St. Clair and what he'd been looking for. He pulled and opened the drawer below the countertop. In the numerous odds and ends of junk, he found a sewing needle stuck into a spool of thread.

"Should I stitch her face up?"

Many times, he'd sewn up injuries of animals on his small ranch and had even done cesareans on sheep from time to time. But he'd never sewn human skin, certainly not on a face like this one. He kept digging in the drawer and found a half full bottle of aspirin and a small bottle of superglue.

Perfect, he thought. He'd used superglue on small cuts for years.

He grabbed the lantern off the table and set it on the wooden arm of the couch where the woman lay. With the wick turned up all the way, the light illuminated her face. Hesitating to start, he went and sat in the chair the old man had died in. He pulled out the drawer in the small table next to the chair. Digging around in the clutter, he found a pair of tweezers. Probably kept this for removing slivers and such, he thought. Then he noticed on the little table the magnifying glass the old man had surely used for reading. He drew a deep breath and returned with both to his patient.

With difficulty, lowering himself to his knees by the couch, he carefully put a little superglue on the tweezers. Starting at one end of the cut, he put a little glue on the skin on one edge. Then he used the tweezers to pull it to the other edge, holding it together for just a couple of seconds. As he followed the cut's path, he told himself that he needed to make a continuous line angle by angle or it wouldn't heal correctly. So he went on a few fractions at a time between each bond.

Finally, he had to stand and stretch because his back and legs were killing him from bending over for so long. The pain in his thigh shot into his hip. He told himself he'd better look it over again as soon as he was done tending to the woman. He limped around the room for a few minutes to loosen up his legs and back and then returned to his work. Now he pulled together the edges of the cut in her lip. He looked down at the wounds and felt good about his efforts to close them. *I hope it works.*

Now he knew he had to start removing some of her clothes to see what her other injuries were. As he tried to pull the sleeve off one of her arms, she moaned so loudly that he decided he'd have to cut her blouse off. He went back to the small table to get the scissors that he'd seen in the drawer. His new little friend laid curled up beside the chair without moving.

Cutting the cloth up the arm from her wrist, he was shocked to see how bruised her wrist and forearm were. He reached the shoulder seam and saw that her shoulder was black and blue too. He snipped through the collar and then started cutting the other sleeve. He immediately saw what he knew was a broken forearm; the end of a bone was causing a big lump under the skin. It was no wonder she'd cried out each time he'd moved her. As he continued cutting up the sleeve and through the collar, he saw she had many more bruises and minor cuts.

Dan started to unbutton the front of Eva's blouse. Oddly, he thought about how long it had been since he and the love of his life had undressed each other in their playful little games before making love. His mind wandered before he snapped back to reality. He realized he didn't need to unbutton it; he'd cut enough of the blouse so that all he had to do was lift the front piece of material off. He had to tug to loosen the cloth from the left side of the woman's chest as it was stuck to her skin by dried blood.

Once that was off, he saw that the left half of her bra was dark red, caked with blood. Slowly, he cut through the middle of the bra and pulled the clean right side off, exposing a beautiful perfectly formed breast and nipple. He couldn't help thinking, *It's been a long, long time since I've been this close to something like this.*

He tried to pull open the left portion of the bra, and she shuddered and moaned with pain. The dried blood had glued the fabric to the skin. He soaked the cloth in the bowl of water and repeatedly wrung it out over the bra cup and surrounding skin. As the fabric got wetter and wetter, he was able to start lifting it off. As he started cleaning the bare blood covered breast, she screamed, and her eyes fluttered.

Dan thought, *Holy cow, she's sensitive. I'm just wiping her skin.* But as he removed more and more blood, he was shocked to see the reason for her pain. He swallowed hard. A deep cut ran from near her armpit and across her nipple, which had been torn halfway off. *Shit! What do I do now? Cut off the rest and close the hole? Try to sew it back on?*

He sat on the floor and stretched out his legs as he let his mind absorb the situation. He asked himself again, *What am I doing?* But he already knew the answer. He had started this venture, and he was going to finish it. He decided what was best would be to try and glue the nipple on.

He applied peroxide and then, with his finger, tipped the nipple over to expose the terrible cut. He dumped more peroxide over the wound and watched it foam. When the foaming stopped, he used the same process he had used on her cheek. Bit by bit, he glued together the edges of the incision that ran across her breast. When he got to the nipple, he applied a little glue all around the jagged bottom edge and pushed it down and held it for a minute.

Ridiculous questions popped into his head, *What if I made the nipple crooked? What if it leans one way or the other?* Then common sense returned. *What am I thinking? What does it matter if she survives with a crooked little nipple?* He smiled just a bit to himself at the thought of this ranch hand putting a crooked nipple on this beautiful woman.

He stood up to stretch his cramping legs and felt pain shot into his hip. He reminded himself he needed to check it out soon. Right now though, his hunger got his attention. He looked at the cans of beans in the cupboard and thought he could eat all three. He told himself he should wait until he was finished tending to the woman. He couldn't resist a jar of honey. He grabbed it and the crackers and spread honey on several of them. He's never tasted anything so wonderful. And the honey gave him an idea.

He knew he could use it to seal her cuts from the outside air so that they could heal and scars would be minimized as much as possible. He dipped his forefinger into the jar of honey and gently rubbed it across the glued together cuts across Eva's cheek and lip. He covered the cuts completely. He did the same with the slash across her breast and around the base of her nipple. He licked his forefinger. No need to waste the delicious honey and set the jar next to the lantern on the couch's wooden arm.

Now Dan turned his attention to Eva's wounded lower half. He used the scissors to cut the right leg of her designer jeans from the bottom up. Although her ankle and foot were black and blue, he didn't feel any bones out of place. He didn't think anything here was broken. When he cut open the other pant leg though, he spotted a bone apparently about to protrude through the skin. There was a lump like the one on her forearm. His heart sank. *Shit! Two broken bones. I never should have started this. Better to have left her near the plane. She'd have died quickly from the cold.*

He took a deep breath and cut the rest of the jean's legs open. He found no other injuries, and when he grabbed the bottom back sides of her jeans and started pulling down, they came off surprisingly easy, exposing long thin legs and small pink lace panties. He examined her waist and saw no blood or serious bruises, so he decided there was no reason to remove her panties. He'd leave her that much dignity, at least.

He again turned his attention to her broken arm. He had spotted a basket of kindling next to the fireplace and found several straight pieces of wood he felt would work for splints. He cut some strips from sheets that lay folded on the couch by her feet. Using both hands, he felt all over her forearm and easily found the bone that was out of place. *Glad she's out. This is going to hurt.*

With one hand, he steadied the back side of her arm while with his other hand he quickly pulled and snapped the bone into place. Eva jerked and cried out. As he gently felt her forearm, Dan thought the bone seemed to be back where it belonged. He splinted the arm to immobilize it and tightly wrapped strips of cloth around it. He tied the loose ends and used stickpins from the drawer to hopefully secure the layers of cloth. Taking up the neatly folded blanket that lay across the back of the couch, he covered the actress from her neck to just below her waist.

Then he stared at her damaged leg. How could he get the femur back into place? If it wasn't done correctly, she'd never walk right again, if they ever got out of here. With a sigh, he concluded he had to try.

He carefully turned her foot so that her toes were straight up in line with her leg. Reaching under her thigh with one hand, he pushed down hard with the other, grimacing at the sound of bone on bone. The cry she uttered was indescribable. Sweaty and dizzy from the effort he'd made, he ran his hands all over the thigh. He discovered there was still a small bump. Meaning, the bone was not completely in place. He again gripped the back of her leg as he pushed down as hard and fast as he could. Again, she cried out in pain. He splinted the leg with the longest pieces of kindling and wrapped and rewrapped it.

Dan picked up the mink coat from the floor and covered the rest of her body. That beautiful mink looked a little rough now. She would be upset. *Yes*, he thought, *Upset if she lives.*

As he turned to go back to the chair, the little dog was standing beside him, wagging his tail.

Dan said, "So you woke up?" Want some water?" As he turned and limped over to the bucket again, he realized it was almost empty. He poured a little water again into the bowl, and the little fella drank it all.

Dan made his way to the door with the bucket and stepped outside, calling his new friend to come, but he just went back and sat by the chair. Dan filled the bucket full of snow and returned it to the counter.

He straightened up and realized he'd been blocking out the severe pain in his own leg. He limped back to the cupboard and took out the old man's half empty aspirin bottle. Before taking any himself, he made his way back to the couch where he gently opened Eva's lips and slipped three aspirin in her mouth. He hoped they would help some with inflammation. He took four tablets out of the bottle for himself, but seeing there were only ten or twelve left, he put two back and swallowed the other two in his hand.

Back again to the motionless woman, he listened to her ragged breathing and thought, That was probably all for nothing. She most likely won't make it. How long she's been out?

Now to take care of himself, he unbuttoned his jeans and pulled them down below his knees, then eased himself into the chair by the table. The swollen skin, surrounding the jagged cut on his leg, was a shocking ugly red color. Dan knew very well what that meant— infection. He considered trying to sew or glue the wound closed but figured it was too late for that. He poured peroxide over the cut and watched it foam profusely. When it was dry, he placed his folded handkerchief over the wound and tied it on with the torn sleeves from the shirt he'd found on the plane.

He thought he should find some of the old man's clothes for Eva. But how could he get them on her with her broken and bruised arms and legs? And then to remove them each time, he would need to look over the cuts. He decided the blanket covering her would have to do for now.

Eventually, he eased his jeans back up, the denim chafing his injured leg. The dried blood made the cloth feel like wood. Noticing the fire had died down, he made himself get up and put three more logs on it. Was the wind roaring more loudly around the cabin? How long had the storm been raging? How long had it been since the plane went down? Two days? Three? Feeling ill and exhausted, he staggered back to the chair, pillowed his head on his crossed arms on the table, and fell asleep.

CHAPTER 5

Meanwhile, back in Los Angeles and even across the nation, the news was full of the story of the plane that was missing with 128 passengers and crew. Of course, the fact that the actress Eva St. Clair had been on board made it an even bigger story. Her manager and personal handlers were harassing the LAX staff and the airline to go look for the missing plane. They didn't seem to grasp the idea that until the blizzard let up, there was no way to send search planes into the air. They were told repeatedly that a ground search in the mountains was also impossible because of strong wind, blowing heavy snow and the rugged terrain. So the nation waited.

Dan was startled awake by a scream. He slowly raised his head, blinking in confusion, and saw that the woman on the couch was apparently trying to sit up. Almost too stiff to get out of his chair, he struggled up and limped across the room. "How do you feel?" Blearily, he realized that had to be the world's stupidest question.

"Who the hell are you?" she shrieked. "Where the hell am I?"

"Do you remember the plane crash?"

She stared at him blankly. "I remember people screaming and crying. And the pilot telling us to bend forward." Her voice was shaky, and her swollen lip made some words sound a little odd. "Did we really crash?"

Pearson explained how he'd found her, the only other survivor, as far as he knew. He told her about pulling her out of the broken fuselage at the last minute before she would have dropped with it, hundreds of feet into a dark canyon. "We could have died in the blizzard. But I saw a light through the snow, and I managed to carry you to this cabin."

She moved feebly on the couch as if to rise, but pain forced her back down again. Her eyes closed.

"What's wrong with me?" she whimpered. "Why does it hurt so much?"

He explained about her injuries and what he had done to treat them, but he wasn't sure how much she understood.

She stirred restlessly under the blanket and her coat. Her eyes opened, and she glowered at him. "Am I undressed?"

He nodded.

"You took my clothes off?"

He explained again that he'd had to cut them off to see the extent of her injuries. She stared into his face, obviously trying to come to terms with the idea of this stranger removing her clothes and probably wondering what he might have done to her besides treating her wounds.

"Believe me," he said, "I didn't have any interest in doing anything but trying to help you."

Angrily she announced, "I want a drink."

Dan filled the metal cup from the bucket on the counter and brought it to her. When he held it out to her, she tried to reach for it, but the pain shooting through her badly bruised wrist and arm prevented it. He slid his arm gently behind her head to raise it and held the cup to her lips so she could drink. She drained the cup.

"Do you want more?"

"I need to pee. Bad."

"In there." He pointed toward the door in the corner.

She tried to ease her body around enough to put her feet on the floor and sit up, but she fell back again. The pain in her bruised and broken limbs was just too much. "I can't get up."

"Of course, you can't. Your legs are broken."

Dan wrapped her in the blanket. Gently he lifted and carried her to the little room where he sat her down on the toilet seat. He went back to get the lantern and set it down on the floor next to her and closed the door, wanting to give her some privacy.

After a few minutes, he realized she was crying. When he couldn't stand it anymore, he stepped closer to the door and asked, "Everything's all right?"

The crying stopped. Silence. "I can't pull my panties down." He stood there not knowing what to say or do. So he said nothing.

She ordered, "Help me."

He thought, *Shit. Pull down this woman's pants?*

He opened the door and looked down at her. She was bent forward, so as to hide her naked body as much as she could, the blanket was laid on the floor around her. He leaned over her and asked if she could stand a little so he could slip her panties down. Then he realized, of course, she couldn't with one broken leg and one bruised so badly. Telling her to put her *good* arm around his neck for balance, he gently pulled her up a bit and slid her panties down her thighs for her. He sat her back down and stepped out, closing the door.

Tired, his leg throbbing, he decided to sit for a minute in his chair. He was almost asleep when he heard her call.

Wearily he dragged himself to the closed door. "Are you okay?"

"Of course, I'm not okay!" she snapped. "I can't pull up my panties, and I can't get up. Does that sound like I'm okay?"

"Do you want help?" he asked foolishly.

"What the hell do you think I need? Jesus Christ!"

Dan grimaced at the words and opened the door. He pulled her panties back on with her, leaning side to side, then picked up the old blanket and wrapped it around her. As he carried her back to the couch, he told her, "You have a very bad mouth."

She didn't reply.

He laid her down. "I should take another look at your wounds."

"You've seen quite enough of my body already! Just put the blanket back on."

He pulled the blanket over her, and retreating to the kitchen area, he muttered, "Fine. I don't care if your nipple rots off. You should be just fine with one."

"What are you talking about? What the hell is wrong with my nipple?"

For the second time, he explained about the horrendous cut on her breast. "I should apply some more honey to it," he said.

She frowned at him without comprehending what he was talking about.

After a long silence, he shrugged and asked if she was hungry. "I'm starving to death."

"Hope you like canned beans or crackers." He held up a can. She replied indignantly, "I'm not going to eat either one!"

"Well," he said with a tired little smile, "I guess you'll be losing some weight."

She snorted. "I need a cigarette badly. Give me one of yours." He waved his hands. "I don't smoke."

Eva complained, "There must be some somewhere in this shithole."

Dan had had enough of her whining. "Lady, this so-called shithole is saving our lives. There's a blizzard out there. The temperature's most likely well below zero. We're only alive because of this little cabin."

He smiled to himself as he remembered spotting a carton of cigarettes on the top shelf of the cupboard.

He wasn't about to tell her, "Now I'm going to open this can of beans. Sure you don't want some?"

"No!" She pouted as she watched him, sitting in the chair and eating out of the can. Her offended expression and her swollen lip gave her a somewhat comical look.

After watching several spoonfuls go into his mouth, she said in a small voice, "Maybe I'll have a spoonful."

He stared at her and then got up and carried the can and spoon over to the couch. He perched on the edge of it and lifted a spoonful of beans to her lips. As she chewed carefully because of her outsize lip, he studied her. Even with the puckered line of the nasty cut across her cheek, he could easily see why the world thought she was one of its most beautiful women. His thoughts drifted to a time, seemingly long ago, of his own beautiful lady and the love they'd shared.

"Give me more."

Dan's attention snapped back to the present. "I thought you didn't like beans."

She said nothing but allowed him to feed her more and more until the can was empty. Then he brought her a cup of water, placed three more aspirin on her tongue, and held the cup so she could drink. Then he brought over the honey jar and explained he needed to rub honey on her check and lip.

"What? Why?"

He explained honey would help prevent infection, keep the cut from drying too fast, and give it more time to heal.

"My face isn't going to be scarred, is it?"

He shrugged a little. "Most likely. The wound was deep and jagged. I did what I could to glue it."

"Glue it! Glue?" she yelled. "What gave you the right to work on my face? Jesus Christ!"

Pearson exploded, "Well, I sure could've just left it to dry wide-open and maybe let infection eat your face away. I could've just let you slip out of that airplane. I should've! I should've just taken care of myself instead of helping a woman who'd never in a million years lift a finger to help me or any other human being."

He took a deep breath and told himself to stop shouting. "And just so you know," he said in a quieter voice, "if you keep taking the Lord's name in vain, I won't help you anymore."

"So you're a Holy Roller," she said contemptuously.

"I don't know what a Holy Roller is, but I try to live a moral life."

"What the hell is that?" the actress asked, but as if she didn't really want to know.

"I try to do unto others as I would have them do unto me. I try to live by the Ten Commandments."

She stared silently into his face.

He added, "I'm guessing you don't know what that means." Still no response but her hostile look. "I should put honey on your face."

As he dipped some honey out of the jar with his forefinger and gently rubbed it on the incision, she flinched, but the pain didn't appear to be severe. As Dan looked closely at her face, he felt good about the job he'd done and thought maybe the scar would just be a thin line.

"Put some of that on my breast," she ordered.

"Please," he prompted.

"What?"

"Say please," he repeated. "Be polite."

"Jesus," she stopped. "Okay, okay. Please."

He pulled the corner of the blanket down and examined the wound and was happy to see there was no discoloration of the nipple itself.

"Thank you, Lord," he said aloud. "What are you thanking him for?"

"Well, everything, but mostly right now, your nipple. I didn't have much hope I could save it the way it was ripped half off, but it already looks like its healing."

As he began to rub honey across her breast and all over the nipple, the moment was not lost on Dan. Unlike when she was unconscious, this seemed like a very personal interaction between them.

He finished as quickly as he could and examined her broken arm. He could see no redness or swelling above or below the cloth strips, binding the splint, and the bruised arm and wrist looked good too. He covered her top half and raised the lower part of the blanket to examine her legs. He couldn't see any sign of infection or worrisome swelling, just black and blue bruised skin everywhere.

As he covered her again, he said, "Everything looks as good as it can."

He noticed she seemed to be asleep. He limped back to his chair, rested his elbow on the table, and propped his head on his hand. Despite the stabbing pain in his leg, he drifted off into a restless sleep.

CHAPTER 6

He awoke to "Hey! Hey, you! Mister!" His head spinning for a minute, Dan looked around and figured out where he was. Rudely calling him "You," Eva demanded to use the bathroom again.

"My name's Dan," he told her.

"And why should I care?"

"Use my name when you talk to me." She snapped, "Fine. Dan."

Again, he carried her into the little room and unwrapped the blanket, helped with her panties, set the lantern down on the floor so she could see, and shut the door. It occurred to him that shutting the door was silly, given what he had had to do for her. It also occurred to him that his leg was getting worse. He was not only in constant pain but given the tightness of his jeans on that leg, it had to be swelling.

"Hey! Hey, you!" the woman called from behind the door of the little room. "Are you out there?"

He didn't answer.

"Hey!" Finally, she said half civilly, "Dan? I'm ready." Responding to her better manners, he opened the door and went through the process of pulling up her panties, wrapping her back in the blanket, carrying her, and getting her settled back on the couch and covered.

Shivering, as chills swept through him, he moved closer to the fireplace. He was sweating, and he knew he had a fever.

"You hungry?"

"No," she snapped. "Are you sure you looked all over for cigarettes? I really need one. Bad."

He shrugged. "I looked everywhere."

He again opened another can of beans and started to eat when she said, "Maybe I could eat some."

He limped over to the couch and again sat beside her as he lifted a spoonful to her lips and kept at it until she finished the can again.

No hunger, he thought. *Right.*

He stood up and walked back to his chair. He sat the empty can on the floor, and his little pal quickly licked it clean and looked up like saying, "Thank you." Dan slowly stroked the top of his head as he wagged his tail.

When Dan unbuttoned his jeans and sat down to inspect his injured leg, he could hardly get his right pant leg down because his thigh was so swollen. The radiating pain, the swelling, the ugly redness around the cut, the red lines running up his leg into his groin— all told him he was in deep trouble. He felt dizzy.

After several minutes of thought, he made himself get up and hobble over to the fireplace where he picked up the iron poker and stuck it into the flames. Going back to his chair was too much of an effort, so he backed up and sat shakily on the edge of the couch's wooden arm to wait for the iron to heat.

Carrie, he thought. He could see her so plainly. *My beautiful girl.* What would happen to her when he was gone? What would happen to their small ranch? *Should've made some arrangements*, he thought hazily. *Thought there was plenty of time.* He must have fallen asleep.

When he woke, he saw the poker was cherry red. Fearing the pain but knowing he had to do this, he shuffled forward and reached for it. As soon as he touched the uninsulated handle end, he jerked his hand back with a grunt of pain. *You idiot. That was dumb. If it's red as a cherry, it's gonna be hot.*

He limped to the kitchen area to get the much used cloth and brought it back to soak it in the snow water in the bucket. Then he folded it over and used it like a pot holder to protect his hand.

Back in the chair by the table, he clutched the poker and closed his eyes, trying to build up his courage. "Now. Do it." He opened his eyes and quickly pressed the hot metal to his infected wound.

Excruciating pain shot through his entire body, and he screamed. He was dimly aware of sizzling and smelled burned flesh. He forced himself to try and hold the poker in place as long as he could. It seemed like forever, but he began shaking so violently that he soon dropped it on the floor, and it rolled out of his reach.

Dan's roar of pain woke Eva, who stared in confusion. She saw him pressing what looked like a glowing metal rod against his bare thigh. In disbelief, she heard what sounded like bacon cooking. A burning smell made her feel sick. The metal bar hit the floor, and Dan toppled sideways onto the table and didn't move. Had he passed out? She bit the top of the blanket and closed her eyes tightly.

After a few minutes, panicking at the thought that maybe Dan was dead and she was alone, Eva opened her eyes.

"Hey!" she called. "Hey, Dan. Dan!"

He stirred. The arm supporting his head moved, and he slowly turned his face toward her.

"Are you okay?"

He nodded and struggled to sit up. Staring down at his burned leg, he told himself, *Well, if that didn't help, nothing will.*

She exclaimed shrilly, "Jesus Christ! I've never seen anything like that!"

Anger swept over him. "Lady, I told you if you took the Lord's name in vain again, I wouldn't help you. You can starve to death as far as I'm concerned and pee your pants too. I'm through helping you."

With a groan, he got to his feet and shuffled over to get the honey jar off the arm of the couch where he'd left it. He leaned against the couch as he reached down and covered his cauterized flesh with the sticky stuff. Just touching his leg hurt something awful, but he forced himself to finish the job.

The woman asked, "Don't I need more honey on my cuts?" Dan didn't say anything, just leaned on the back of the couch panting. "Dammit, Dan, don't I need honey on my cuts?" He took a deep breath. "What did I tell you?"

She sounded irritated, "Oh hell, what do you want me to do?"

"First, no more swearing. And you could ask for forgiveness."

"I don't know how to do that," she frowned. "I haven't been around a church since I was a little girl. I don't even know if I believe there is a god."

"You better believe there is. It's why you're still alive."

Her thoughts flooded back to a time as a little girl, growing up in Chicago, a mother who was involved with the theater and the arts, a father who told people where to put their money. She always felt she had a perfect childhood, everything she wanted, and a mother who felt she should be entering beauty contests because everyone said she was just so cute. She could not even remember how many contests and how many she had won, how many dancing and singing lessons she had gone to. All the while, her mother was telling her that she and her father were doing it for her.

She also remembered a time when they would go to church as a family, "if we had nothing else to do" and remembered learning of Christ and his death on the cross and had always felt sorry for how he had been treated.

There were many things she did not understand and wanted to ask, but by the time she was a preteen, her father had left home, and her mother no longer went to church.

CHAPTER 7

The next few years were not happy times as her mother was bitter about her father leaving and moving away, leaving her to raise Eva by herself. At the same time, her mother was pushing her more and more into acting classes and less into beauty contests.

By twelve, Eva had already done four national commercials, and her mother decided they must move to Los Angeles to be "where it's at."

Moving there separated her from the only childhood friend she had ever had, Emma. She was the one and only person Eva could talk to, to share feelings and dreams with.

After the move to LA, acting and commercials just seemed to disappear. For many months, she did not go to any screenings, and her mother talked of being short of money and not being able to buy things or pay the rent. Her mother said her father was no longer sending money, and she had no idea where he was. She remembered missing her father.

Even though not really close, he had always been good to her and tried to always give her what she wanted. She had not talked to him for many months at that time. She tried once when her mother was gone somewhere to call her best friend Emma. But the phone had been disconnected. She never talked to her again.

Then the big break at fourteen with a part in a movie where she didn't talk much but was in many scenes and after it showed, the calls started coming.

By sixteen, she was on her own because she felt her mother didn't understand her or know how to get her the best parts. A man had approached her on her last film part and said he wanted to be her agent and had big plans for her, would make her a star! That also began her first sexual experience with a man, a much older man, maybe in his late forties.

She had often thought back over the years of her first time living with a man and decided it surely had nothing to do with love. It was a relationship, sadly, that both got something out of. True to his word, he did get better and better parts for her in better and bigger movies, so her career was going straight up at age twenty.

That was when, during the filming of a movie, she met Tommy. Tommy did take her heart, and for the first time, she had feelings for a man other than her father. Eva wanted to be with him, shared going places, telling him about her day, and even thought about a family.

That all came crashing down two years later when he informed her he had fallen in love with another woman. Eva was crushed. She had no idea, thought they were happy together, thought he was as happy as she was. Her life had fallen apart.

Over the next almost twenty years, she had numerous *men* in her life, but she never allowed herself to ever again have feelings for any of them. She was never going to be hurt as she had been. Never again.

Jolted back to the present, Eva said, "So what? How—"

Dan eased himself down onto the arm of the couch. "Just say to yourself, 'Forgive me, Lord, for my sins.'"

Eva said, "All my sins?"

He gave her a weak smile. "Well, maybe he could not handle that much at one time. Just start with forgiveness for using his name in vain."

After a silence, she said, "Okay, I did. What about my cuts?" As he gently applied honey to the olive skin of her face and breast, she felt his finger trembling. That and the sweat she saw on his forehead told her how ill he must be. In spite of her self-centeredness, she was beginning to realize that this man of strong will and beliefs had done everything he could to help her, despite his own injuries. She wondered about him. She was helpless and completely reliant on this man who she did not know anything about.

She blurted, "I bet you have never been this close to a black woman before."

Dan had pulled an old chair beside the couch to sit on while he worked on her and upon her saying that he yelled out, "You're black?" And with that, Dan pulled back as if touching something that burned his fingers. As he pulled back laughing, he lost his balance on the chair and fell backward onto the floor, reeling in pain from his leg. The little dog had raised his head and was looking at them.

Laughing, Dan picked himself up as she was also laughing. Giving a snort of laughter, "You'd lose that bet. My wife had very much the same skin color you have."

"Was she black?"

He shrugged. "I never asked."

"What do you mean you never asked?"

"I never thought of it as she was beautiful on the outside as well as the inside and where she came from didn't matter to me."

"Ha! I can't believe that. Black and white matter because they're different, and I sure wouldn't—" she stopped.

"Be with a white man?" he said, finishing her thought for her.

She shook her head.

As he finished applying honey to her nipple, "Have you ever been this close to a white man before?"

"Hell, no!"

He scowled at her for swearing. "That's easy to understand coming from that cesspool you call a life where your kind just use each other for what you can get. Never giving, always taking, and never knowing the true relationship between a man and a woman other than your own personal satisfaction and gain."

"I have cared for a man," she protested. "I loved him."

"Did he do things for you other than use you?"

"Yes, he did."

Pearson asked, "What did he do for you?" When she did not answer, he went on, "In your world, people don't even know how to treat each other with respect. You call each other names and treat each other as objects."

"We do not!" If she could have turned her back on him, she would have.

"What did your lover call you? Did he use your name or honey or...? Did he call you what I hear on TV...bitch?"

"No one calls me bitch! I am beautiful. I am loved by people all over the world. I can have anything I want. What right do you have to talk to me like that?"

He replied that he had peace with himself, something she would never understand.

"Yes, I know. Your moral life and living however."

"By the Ten Commandments."

"Whatever."

Dan went back to the chair by the table where the old man had died and laboriously bent to pick up his jeans from the floor. He took the scissors and cut down along the seam of the right leg from the crotch to the knee. As the little dog watched him, you could see he knew and understood what this new master was going through. He stood up and put his head on the man's leg as if to say, "I understand."

"I bet you don't even know the Ten Commandments."

"Yes, I do. I learned them when I was little."

"So say them for me," he mocked her.

"I don't have to."

"Because you don't know them."

"Yes, I do. 'Thou shall not kill.'"

He pushed his feet through his jeans and gingerly pulled them up. He never would have got them on if he had not cut the leg. He focused back on their conversation.

"Yes, and what else?"

"You shouldn't screw around."

"Yes." He rephrased it for her, "'Thou shall not commit adultery,' and?" She said nothing, and he said, "It's very easy to live by the Ten Commandments."

She sneered, "Oh sure, if you're a Holy Roller and don't want to have any fun."

"Oh no, it doesn't say anywhere in the Bible you can't have fun. Quite the opposite. It says, 'You shall enjoy life and the things around you.' Do you want to hear them all?" When she didn't respond, he began, "The first commandment is 'I am the Lord thy God. You shall have no other gods before me.'"

"What other god would we have?"

"In biblical times, people worshipped many different gods. The second commandment says, 'You should not worship false prophets or idols. I am the only God. Throw away all your false idols.' Do you know what number three is? It is your favorite, 'You shall not take the name of the Lord in vain.'"

She looked away without responding.

"Number four is simple, 'Remember Sunday and keep it holy.' Remember number five?"

She shook her head.

"'Honor your father and mother.'"

"A lot, you know," she said. "You never knew my father or mother or the life I had."

He answered, "It means that we should always treat our parents with love and respect because without them, we, of course, would not be here. Commandment six is the one you know: 'Thou shall not kill.' How easy can that be to live by that commandment? Don't kill someone? And you know number seven also: 'Thou shall not commit adultery.' Again, very easy, you don't mess around! It seems most of the world has forgotten this one. Number eight is also very easy to follow: 'Thou shall not steal.' Don't take something that does not belong to you."

"What number was that?"

When he repeated, "Number eight." She said, "Only two left."

"Yes, number nine is 'You shall not bear false witness against your neighbor.' You know what that means?"

She said, "It is confusing."

"It simply means you should not tell a lie about another person and what that person may have said or done. And the last one, any guesses?"

Eva heaved a sigh, "No, let's have it."

"'You should not covet your neighbor's things.' House, wife, belongings—anything that is your neighbors'.'"

"Well, that just says the same thing as the last one."

"Kind of. They both mean we should treat others as we want them to treat us and what they have we should not ask for because it is theirs. See, the Commandments are very easy to live by!"

Silence fell. Dan didn't know if she was thinking about what they had been talking about. He hoped so. He let his eyes close and felt himself about to drift away.

"I'm hungry," she said suddenly. "And I'm tired, and pretty soon, I'll need to go to the bathroom again."

His head jerked, and he opened his eyes. "You need, you want, you, you, you!" He scooped up a cup of icy water from the bucket by the fireplace. He put the last two aspirin in her mouth and raised her head so she could drink the whole cup. He brought the final can of beans from the cupboard, thinking vaguely, *Why am I not hungry?*

The chills had gone, and now he felt warm all over and realized his fever was rising. He limped back to the couch, perched on the edge, and fed her the whole can of beans.

She surprised him by demanding more, "I told you I was hungry. I bet you ate all the rest when I was sleeping!" She didn't seem to be joking. She must have forgotten he'd been cauterizing his leg with a hot poker while she was sleeping.

He stared at her in disbelief, so much for his lessons about how to treat people.

"Whatever," she said. "Bathroom."

As he watched the little dog again walk over and clean the can with his long tongue, he limped over to the counter and poured some dog food into the bowl, and his new buddy started to eat.

Resentfully he picked her up once more, and he carried her once again to the little room and got her settled on the pot. He was feeling weak and wondered how much longer he would be able to lift her. He sat on the couch as he waited for her to finish and immediately dozed off. He woke to the sound of crying and walking to the door asked what was wrong.

"I'm done."

"Fine." Opening the door, he went to again go through the actions of pulling her panties on.

Eva stopped him by saying, "There's more."

"What more?"

She started crying again and standing back up.

He said, "What's wrong now?"

"I need to wipe!"

And he said, "Shit!"

And crying, she said, "Exactly!"

He couldn't help laughing a little. It was the last thing he wanted to do, but he wiped her butt as she leaned heavily against him. Picking her up, he carried her back to the couch. As he sat back again in his chair, he thought to himself, *Come on, Dan, you really need to empty that pot under the seat now. But how can I? I can't even throw it out of the door.*

He remembered the wall of snow blocking access to the porch and stayed where he was, too weak to try and kick the snow out of the way. These were his thoughts as he again fell asleep.

CHAPTER 8

Sometime later, she awakened, looking across the room, saw that he was naked, except for his shorts, and was giving himself a sponge bath, dipping in a bowl of water and rubbing his arms, neck, and chest, returning the sponge each time, squeezing, and cleaning his legs. Observing this, she startled him by saying, "I am sweaty and dirty also."

He stood up, walking over to her, he again dipped the cloth in the water and began to gently rub her forehead, good cheek, and neck, avoiding her cut cheek. He continued on to her shoulders and around her breast and tummy, and as he hesitated for a moment, she started to spread her legs apart, and he jerked back saying "Shit, it's hot in here."

Taking the bowl back to the kitchen, his thoughts were racing everywhere, and she said, "Aren't you going to finish washing me?"

Dan didn't know how much time had passed. She had just told him she wanted her clothes put on, and he replied, "You have no clothes. I had to cut them off you." Then he finally realized something was missing: the constant roar of the wind.

"Listen, I think the wind's gone down. Maybe the storm's over.

Somebody'll find us soon." At least, he hoped.

He made his way to the fireplace and put the last logs he had carried in on the small fire remaining and thought after a little nap he would try and figure out how to dig into the snowbank and find some more firewood and let the dog out. Heck, he must have to go by now.

Where would he put the snow? Those were his thoughts as he sat back down in the chair and leaned back. He felt very, very hot and knew his fever was going up. He was so hot. Maybe he'd cool off by crawling into the snow. He wondered how high his fever was. Pillowing his head on his hands, his mind wandered and wondered if anyone would ever find them, or was he to die in this little cabin in the middle of nowhere? *Will Carrie ever know what happened to me? Jose, take care of my baby.*

Eva woke him by shouting, "What is that? Dan, wake up! Listen! Is someone coming? Did they find us?"

Pearson heard a distant rumble. As it came closer and closer, he decided it must be a motor, but he was too tired and sick to get up and see. Sometime after that, he thought he saw the door swinging open and snow pouring into the cabin. He became aware of what sounded like excited voices: a dog barking. Was he dreaming? Everything faded into blackness.

He became aware of very bright lights. It seemed to him that, for the first time in who knew how many days, he was lying flat on his back and was moving. He thought he heard a familiar woman's voice saying, "I want…" It faded out. Groggily he wondered, "What do you want now, Eva?"

Eva kept her eyes shut against the harsh lights overhead. She heard a man asking in a hushed voice, "What happened to her face? She won't be modeling or acting again."

An authoritative sounding man shushed him and said, "I've sent for Dr. O'Donnel. He's the best plastic surgeon in the area. If anyone can fix her, he can!"

Eva felt the blanket that had covered her for so long, being lifted off. She shivered as the air brushed her almost naked body. She was only protected by her panties and the wraps around her forearm and thigh.

The second man inquired, "What happened to her? Domestic abuse? Car accident? Look at the bruises all over her body. Cut those bandages and let's see what we're dealing with."

As she was rushed to the emergency room, the doctor on duty, a man of many years and close to retirement, stared down at this woman as the nurses were cutting off the blanket that had been wrapped around her many times. And as they did, he saw this naked woman, except for her panties and a leg and arm wrapped up in tight clothing, the black and blue bruises all over her body said, "What has this woman been through?"

The nurse, attending to Eva, stated, "Have you been living under a rock? She has been missing for a week in a plane crash where all the passengers died except for her and a man."

As someone gently moved her arm, Eva opened her eyes and blinked up at a gray haired man dressed in blue scrubs. A man of many years and close to retirement stared down at her. Beside him, a nurse was carefully cutting through the layers of cloth strips, covering the splints on her arm.

"Plane crash," Eva managed to croak.

Her mouth and throat were so dry she could hardly talk. Someone held a straw to her mouth. She winced as the end of it poked her swollen lip, but she sucked the refreshing water eagerly.

"Plane crash. You must have heard about it on the news."

"Ma'am, who did this?" asked the doctor as he looked at the kindling wood splints.

Instead of answering, she demanded haughtily, "Do you know who I am?"

"Some actress, they tell me," he answered casually.

She glared up at him. "I'm Eva St. Clair. I'm one of the most famous people you'll ever see."

He seemed unimpressed.

"I've had a terrible time. I've been stuck in a cabin with this barbarian for days. He took away my clothes, and he hardly fed me."

Someone spread a deliciously warm blanket over everything but her broken leg.

"And he kept me wrapped up in a rough smelly blanket."

The doctor commented to the nurse, who was now cutting through the wrappings on the actress's leg, "Well, looks to me like this barbaric man took better care of her than she knows. These splints didn't jump on all by themselves."

Eva closed her eyes again as he pulled a bright light down closer to her face. He asked someone to hand him a magnifying glass, and Eva felt his breath on her face as he leaned closer. "What is that paste that is all over these cuts? See how it's flaking?"

Eva felt his gloved hand run lightly along the cut across her cheek.

A nurse said, "Looks just like honey that my kids leave on the plate overnight."

"Hmm, honey," said the doctor thoughtfully. "Used to keep the skin moist maybe. And look how nicely the cut here and the one on her breast are healing. But I don't see any stitches. What did the guy use?"

The portable X-ray machine had just finished its work and was being rolled away as the images were coming through on the big wall screen.

"Ms. St. Clair," the doctor said, "it looks to me like that fracture in your arm was perfectly set and is starting to heal already, judging by the calcification setting in the crack. And the more severe one in your leg looks good too. An orthopedic surgeon will take a look at them, of course. A plastic surgeon will be in to examine your face too, though personally, I don't think he'll have much to do." He patted her shoulder and left the room.

She heard him speak to someone right outside the door. "Ah, Dr. O'Donnel, she's all yours."

"She's very famous, you know," a younger voice said eagerly. "Her work depends on her face. How bad is it? I heard she's cut up pretty badly. I've order her prepped for surgery."

"Well, young man, you might have a different opinion after you've seen her. I don't think there's much for you to do, probably going to want to cancel those orders."

CHAPTER 9

E va did not have plastic surgery, and doctors did not reset the bones in her arm and leg. She spent weeks recuperating out of sight of cameras and the public. Her manager did several interviews about her ordeal and based on what the actress had told him, spun a tale of how badly she had been treated by the stranger in the cabin.

One day, after watching on TV, a particularly vicious version of the story her manager had concocted, Eva mused to her assistant, Mariah, "I wonder what happened to that man who was in the cabin with me? He was hurt very bad in the leg." She shuddered as she remembered how Dan had burned his flesh with the hot poker. She pushed that picture out of her mind. "You'd think he would have sold his story of his days alone with Eva St. Clair to some tabloid."

"I haven't heard anything about him," answered Mariah without much interest. "Maybe he died."

At her sixty day checkup with the plastic surgeon, Eva asked if the scar on her face would be visible for the rest of her life.

Dr. O'Donnell reassured her, "Somehow, the edges of the cuts came together and have healed unbelievably well. And that special cream I gave you looks to be doing its job. Only time will tell, but I think you may only end up with a minor line which can be covered with makeup."

The orthopedist asked how her arm was, and she said there was very little pain, sometimes when she moved it too fast or twisted it badly, but all in all, it felt good. "And your leg?" he asked.

"There's hardly any pain," she said. "I just want to be off the *goddamn* crutches." And as she said that, thoughts came flooding back to her about this man that had helped her and told her about taking the Lord's name in vain, and suddenly, she felt alone and unsure of the world around her.

One day after weeks later, as she was putting on her makeup in front of her mirror, Eva said to Mariah, "I'm very lucky. I can barely even see where the cut was and a little makeup, and it's all gone!"

Mariah said, "Yes, you are very lucky, and I have been wondering about that a lot and just how lucky you are, or did that man in the cabin have a lot to do with it?"

Eva waved her hand dismissively, saying, "How could he?" Then she remembered the many times Dan had gently applied honey to her cuts and her nipple, and, yes, the nipple was just a little crooked, but already Dr. O'Donnel said it was very lucky to be there at all. It should have been gone! She thought of her conversation with Dan. He was different from any man she'd ever known.

Later she had Mariah drive her to the hospital. Eva explained, "I have to know what happened to this man. I can't get him out of my mind."

"What the hell is wrong with you?" asked her assistant. "You're lucky to be alive. You're lucky this man didn't rape you or something."

Eva shocked herself by yelling, "No! He would never do anything like that. That is not the kind of man he was."

At the hospital's information desk, Eva said to the woman seated behind the counter, "I am looking for a doctor, an older man that worked the ER three months ago!" She gave the woman the date.

The woman, staring up star struck, said, "You're Eva St. Clair!"

"Yes," Eva said somewhat impatiently. "I am. I want to thank this doctor for what he did. Can you find out who it is?"

After several phone calls, the woman wrote the name and number on a piece of paper and handed it to the actress.

"They never give out phone numbers like this, but this lady in the business office remembered your story from the news. His name's Dr. Ronald Jackson. He's retired now." Shyly, she asked Eva for her autograph and the actress obliged.

On the way to their car, she pulled out her cell phone and quickly dialed the number on the piece of paper, and as it was ringing, she hung up. Mariah said, "No answer?"

Eva said, "No."

On the drive home, again, her thoughts were on this man and the doctor she had to talk to. Again, she dialed up the number, and she could not believe how nervous she was. She had not been this nervous since her first stage performance. A woman answered the phone, and Eva said, "Is Dr. Jackson there?"

The other woman said, "Can I tell him who is calling?" Eva said, "Yes, it's Eva St. Clair."

The woman said, "One moment, please."

A short time later, a man said, "Ms. St. Clair, how are you?" Eva said she was fine and would love to see him and ask a few questions about her hospital stay.

Dr. Jackson said, "My wife and I were just going out to dinner, would you join us?"

Eva started to say no, she could not. She had places to be and then stopped, said, "Sure, where are you going?"

After Dr. Jackson had given her the name and address, they googled it to see how far it was and if they had time to go home and change clothes or not and finding the location decided it was a long drive and they would just get there in time.

Mariah protested, saying she did not want to go, but short of catching a cab home alone, she would come.

It was a very nice small steak house they entered and gave her name to the woman at the door. She was told Dr. Jackson was waiting for her and showed her to his table. Seeing him again brought back that afternoon in the hospital, and all the people yelling and running around, trying to help her and his calm voice saying all would be okay and giving instructions where to take her.

As he introduced his lovely wife, Eva introduced Mariah as her good friend.

When seated, Dr. Jackson said, "Eva, may I stand by you and look closer?"

And she said, "Yes, of course."

As he gazed into her face carefully, looking at the cheek where that nasty cut had been, he could find no sign of it, remarking, "Ms. St. Clair, this is amazing. It's like you were never cut!"

"Yes, I was very lucky."

Pausing for a moment, Dr. Jackson said, "Yes, you had some luck, but you had someone work on you that very much knew what he was doing." He went on to explain that Dr. O'Donnel, after reviewing the cuts, had come to the conclusion the cuts had been glued shut, better than the plastic surgeon could ever do. The honey application was pure genius and from someone who understood cuts and healing. And as far as the broken bones go, there sure may have been some luck as no man without X-rays or medical knowledge should have been able to set them as he did. Dr. Jackson went on, "I sure would have liked to talk to him about it."

She was afraid to ask. Then she did, "Did he die?"

"Not that I know. I helped work on him, and I couldn't believe the pain this man must have endured. He had blood poisoning from that horrific injury to his leg. How he could cauterize it himself is beyond me. We put him on a strong IV antibiotic and fluids and hoped for the best. He was severely dehydrated, and his system was starting to shut down from not only the fever, but also it appeared he had not eaten for days."

Eva remembered accusing him of eating all the beans and giving her little and now felt the pain of realizing this man must have let her have all the food. Now she felt ashamed. Dr. Jackson went on to say he did not understand how she was able to keep a fever from overtaking her body with her numerous cuts and broken bones.

Eva explained Dan continuously fed her aspirin. She then said, "So why didn't it keep his fever in check also?"

Dr. Jackson shrugged. "He must not have been taking as many, and his injury was worse."

Eva's thoughts returned to the cabin and the last time he had given her two aspirin, the last ones in the bottle, and she wondered, "Could this man have saved them all for me? If he did that with the food, would he not with the aspirin?"

They ate in silence for a time, and her thoughts never left that little cabin and this very strong man she somehow felt an attachment to and knew she needed to see him again, to talk to him, to know his life, and, yes, as she now knew more than ever, to thank him.

Dr. Jackson went on to say that after treating the man, the next day, he was scheduled off for three days and, when he returned, found out the man had checked himself out, calmly stating he wanted to go home to his own doctors.

Eva said, "Do you know his name? Or where he is from?"

Dr. Jackson said, "No, I don't remember it, but know he is from a small town one hundred miles north or so."

Eva said, "I feel I must thank this man. Can you get me his name and address please?"

Dr. Jackson said, "Yes, I have some connections still there. I will make some calls."

At that time, Eva gave Dr. Jackson her phone number and thanked him for all he had done.

They made their way to the car.

Mariah said, "Eva, you have changed and are acting different." Eva said, "What do you mean?"

And she went on to say, "Well, you're trying to quit smoking, and you are thanking Dr. Jackson twice! You never, in all the time, I have known you thanked anybody for anything!"

Eva protested, saying, "Yes, I have," but thought to herself, *Is Mariah right?*

CHAPTER 10

Later that night, at her on-again-off-again boyfriend Leroy's apartment, she stated to light a cigarette and then remembered what Mariah had said. Her assistant had noticed she had been trying to give up cigarettes. As she stubbed out her unsmoked cigarette and headed to the kitchen for a drink, Leroy yelled out, "Hey, bitch, grab me a beer on your way back!"

She automatically started to answer, "Sure, hon—" and it hung there, and that little chat in the cabin came flooding back of how she would answer to a name that was not hers and how her life was a cesspool, according to Dan. She whirled around and headed out the door. Sprawled on the couch in front of the televised football game, Leroy didn't even notice.

Driving herself home, she couldn't help thinking all the things the man had said to her again, his gentle touch, and she knew a man who had cared for her more than he had cared for himself. She had to see this man. She had to know more about this man.

The phone woke her the next morning, and as she answered it half asleep, the voice on the other end said, "Eva, this is Dr. Jackson, and I have this man's name and address."

Immediately, Eva was awake and looked for pen and paper as she nervously wrote.

"The name is Dan Pearson, and he is from Shandon." Eva thanked him over and over before she hung up.

Dr. Jackson had said, "If you talk to Mr. Pearson, would you call me back and tell me how he is doing?"

She promised to do so.

She could not get back to sleep. She showered and knew there was only one thing to do. She must go to this little town and find him to see him, to thank him. She called Mariah as she was leaving LA, telling her of her plans, and Mariah asked if she had lost her mind and what the hell did she think she was doing?

Eva said calmly, "Mariah, I have to do this. I have to have answers."

During that four-hour drive by herself, *Yes, by herself,* she thought, "*I can drive and used to drive, but since I became* famous, *someone has always driving me*. But she had kept up her license just so she would not have to depend on someone else if she didn't want to.

Her mind was flooded with thoughts and emotions as to what she would see, what she would say to this man that most likely hated her after what she and her manager had told the media. No, she decided he was not the kind of person who hated people. That was clear by the way he had treated the old homeless woman at the airport. Yes, the airport!

Now this new revelation, this man, Dan, who had taken care of her, saved her face, and, yes, she knew saved her life, was the same man who had helped the old woman when they went to the airport. She thought of that and remembered her and her group laughing at the scene. She now caught herself feeling bad about how she had looked upon this helpless old woman.

She was jolted back to the present, wondering how she would talk to Dan or even start the conversation. Or would he even talk to her? All these questions flooded her mind as she pulled into a convenience store in the small town and went inside to ask if someone could fill her gas tank.

"Sorry, ma'am," said the elderly man behind the counter. "We don't do that. This isn't a full service station. They don't even exist anymore." Then he took a closer look at her. "Are you Eva St. Clair?" When she admitted she was, he smiled, "I'll be happy to fill your car." When she paid, she asked if he knew a Dan Pearson. "Oh sure, lived here all his life."

She cleared her suddenly dry throat. "Can you give me directions to his house?"

"Yeah. He's got a small ranch just outside of town. Go right six blocks. Take a left, then go nine or ten blocks till you come to a little road, leading to a ranch house."

She drove the first leg, and turning, she went how many blocks? She was not sure. Stopping at a stop sign, there was an old Mexican woman standing on the corner and rolling down her window, said, "Ma'am, ma'am. Can you tell me where Mr. Pearson lives?"

"Yes, but no one is at home. They're all gone to Mr. Pearson's funeral."

Eva's face dropped, and she said in a low voice, "Funeral?" The old woman told her, "Yes, Mr. Pearson at the graveyard.

Just turn right for three blocks, and you will run right into it."

As Eva thanked her and started to turn, she could not hold back the tears. She would never see this man who saved her life, never talk to him, never ask him why he had saved her, and never thank him. The tears just kept coming as she drove slowly toward the graveyard, not knowing why she was even going there. She parked at the end of a long line of cars and just sat there as she looked at the large group of people in the middle of the graveyard.

She did not even remember getting out of the car but found herself walking toward this group of people and trying to control the tears that were still running down her cheeks—the cheek this man had repaired with his gentle touch, and now he was gone!

She stood a short distance from the group of mourners, not hearing what the minister was saying until a name penetrated her consciousness, "And now, we commit our brother in Christ, Andrew Pearson, to his final rest. None of us will ever forget this wonderful father, grandfather, friend, and neighbor."

Eva's startled thoughts spun wildly. "What did he say? Mr. Andrew Pearson? Not Dan Pearson?"

As people began moving away from the grave, she peered past and around them. Finally she spotted a tall man standing with a small dog by his side with his arm around a young girl. She made her way through the crowd, and there he was. The man she couldn't get out of her thoughts. He was here. He was alive!

And then, he turned and saw her. He gave her a small smile. She walked over to his side, and he slipped his arm around her waist. He bent to kiss her forehead. The puzzled girl leaned against her father on the left, and the tearful but smiling woman leaned against him on the right, both drawing strength from him.

Eva whispered, "Thank you, Dan."

"When that final door closes on life and
your making that last ride in the hearse, may not
be the best time to ask for directions."

Douglas Alan

ABOUT THE AUTHOR

This is Mr. Douglas Alan's first book written where he lives on a ranch in the western Dakota with his wife of forty-five years.